A Cookie for Santa

Stephanie Shaw and Illustrated by Bruno Robert

PUBLISHED BY SLEEPING BEAR PRESS

In memory of my father, Capt. Hugh E. Shaw.
—S.G.S.

To Séraphine and Asphodèle
—B.R.

Sleeping Bear Press™

315 E. Eisenhower Pkwy., Suite 200
Ann Arbor, MI 48108
www.sleepingbearpress.com

Printed and bound in the United States.
10 9 8 7 6 5 4 3 2 1

Library of Congress Cataloging-in-Publication Data

Shaw, Stephanie (Stephanie Gale), 1950-
A cookie for Santa / written by Stephanie Shaw ;
illustrated by Bruno Robert.
pages cm
Summary: "Anticipating he will be eaten, a gingerbread boy cookie nervously awaits Santa's arrival. When rough-housing puppies threaten Christmas morning joy, the cookie comes to the rescue, earning the Night Watchman job at the North Pole" -- Provided by publisher.
ISBN 978-1-58536-883-9
[1. Stories in rhyme. 2. Cookies--Fiction. 3. Christmas--Fiction. 4. Dogs--Fiction.
5. Animals--Infancy--Fiction. 6. Santa Claus--Fiction.]
I. Robert, Bruno, 1967- illustrator. II. Title.
PZ8.3.S5347Coo 2014
[E]--dc23
2014004480

'Twas the night before Christmas,
And there on a plate,
Was a Gingerbread Boy
Awaiting his fate.

The children had baked him
And dressed him with care,
Using currants for eyes
And icing for hair.

They knew that St. Nick,
With his overstuffed pack,
Would be sorely in need
Of a fine midnight snack.

The Christmas tree sparkled.
Strands of lights glimmered.
Snowflakes and garlands all
Glittered and shimmered.

The Gingerbread Boy,
Despite all this beauty,
Nervously pondered
His Christmas Eve duty.

Later that evening
When he'd be devoured
Would he be brave?
Or a crumbling coward?

Bursting into the room,
"Is ALL THIS for us?"
Two puppies came bounding
And started a fuss.

They leapt and they snapped
And they played tug-of-war.
They pounced and they pawed
And they ripped and they tore!

The Gingerbread Boy thought
"Oh, what can be done?
These puppies are having
The wrong kind of fun!"

He knew to save Christmas
He'd need to take action.
"I'll make myself into
A Doggie Distraction."

"Come, Rascal! Come, Rowdy!"
He called them by name.
"I'll show you a much better
Christmas Eve Game."

"A biscuit," they barked
With howling dog joy.
"And one that can talk.
It's a Gingerbread Boy!"

And what he did next
Made those naughty pups stop.
"Look at me!" Cookie cried.
"I can spin like a top!"

He twirled and he spun
Until he was dizzy
Keeping exuberant
Puppies quite busy.

Tails wagging, tongues drooling,

The pups were entranced

While the Gingerbread Boy

Deeeeeeeliciously danced.

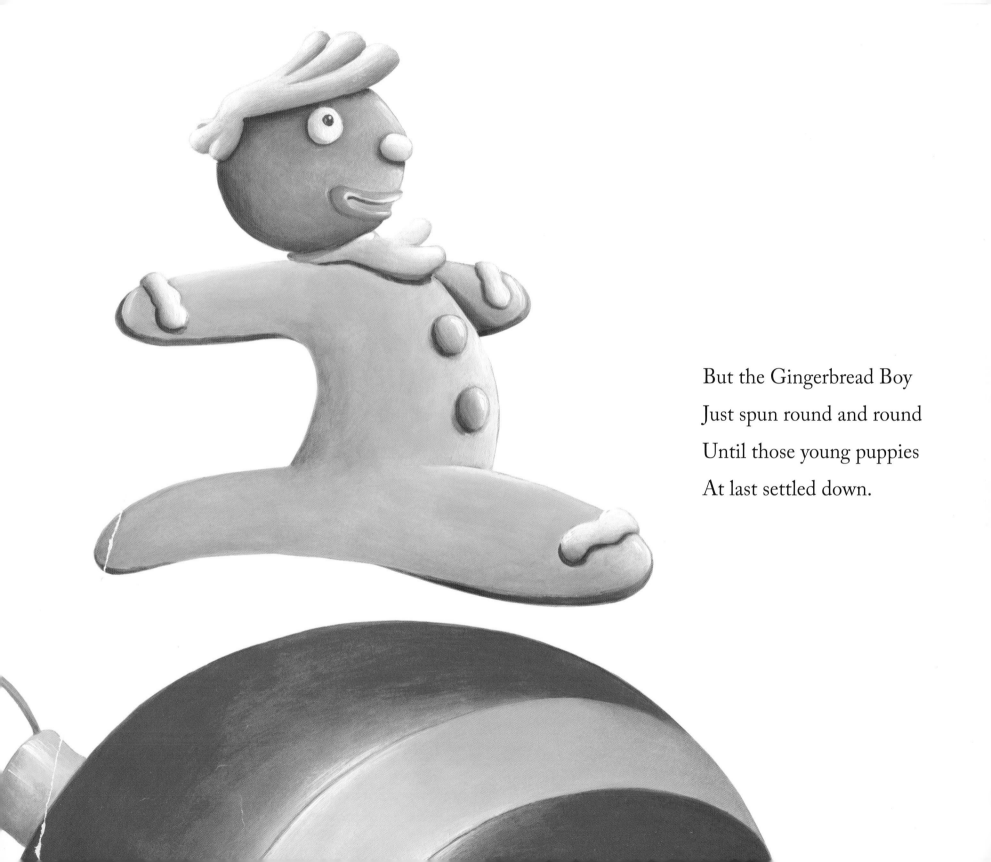

But the Gingerbread Boy
Just spun round and round
Until those young puppies
At last settled down.

A jingling of Christmas bells
Came from outside.
"It's Santa!" the pups yipped.
"Woof! Let's go hide!"

Would Santa Claus start
With his legs or his head?
Would he nibble his arms
Or his buttons instead?

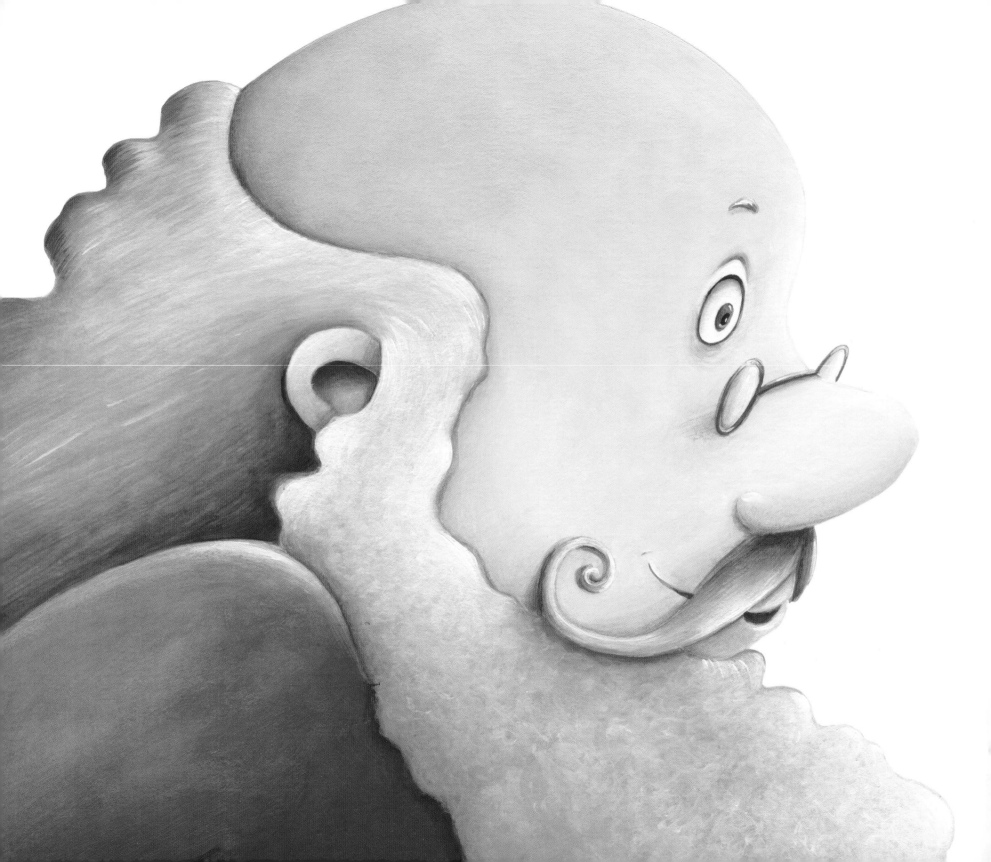

Santa said, "On my radar
There was trouble reported.
Can you lend me a hand
Getting all of this sorted?"

The Gingerbread Boy
Helped jolly St. Nick.
With morning approaching
They had to be quick.

When the work was all done

Cookie climbed on the dish.

He looked to the stars

And made one Christmas wish.

Then he heard Santa say...

"We make a great team.
Come hop in my sleigh.
There are more homes to visit
Before Christmas Day.

And I need you for duty
Up at the North Pole."
Toy soldiers saluted
And gave a drum roll.

Christmas morning the children

Found gifts and a note.

In festive green ink

Santa Claus wrote:

I've searched the world over

And found at this stop

The perfect Night Watchman

To mind my toy shop.

And as for those pups

That created a mess,

I've left something special

For them. Can you guess?

Gift Certificate
Good to the Bone Puppy Obedience School